A VERY SPECIAL WISH
A Collection of Stories to Share

LITTLE TIGER PRESS
An imprint of Magi Publications
1 The Coda Centre, 189 Munster Road,
London SW6 6AW
www.littletigerpress.com

First published in Great Britain 2008
This volume copyright
© Magi Publications 2008
Cover illustration copyright
© Frank Endersby 2008

THE WISH CAT
Ragnhild Scamell
Illustrated by Gaby Hansen
First published in Great Britain 2001
by Little Tiger Press
An imprint of Magi Publications
Text copyright © Ragnhild Scamell 2001
Illustrations copyright © Gaby Hansen 2001

THE VERY BUSY DAY
Diana Hendry
Illustrated by Jane Chapman
First published in Great Britain 2001
by Little Tiger Press
An imprint of Magi Publications
Text copyright © Diana Hendry 2001
Illustrations copyright © Jane Chapman 2001

THE MOST PRECIOUS THING
Gill Lewis
Illustrated by Louise Ho
First published in Great Britain 2006
by Little Tiger Press
An imprint of Magi Publications
Text copyright © Gill Lewis 2006
Illustrations copyright
© Louise Ho 2006

MOUSE, MOLE AND THE
FALLING STAR
A H Benjamin
Illustrated by John Bendall-Brunello
First published in Great Britain 2002
by Little Tiger Press
An imprint of Magi Publications
Text copyright
© A H Benjamin 2002
Illustrations copyright
© John Bendall-Brunello
2002

A Very Special Wish

A Collection of Stories to Share

LITTLE TIGER PRESS
London

Contents

The Wish Cat

Ragnhild Scamell

illustrated by Gaby Hansen

Holly's house had a cat flap.
It was a small door in the
big door so a cat could come
and go.

But Holly didn't have a cat.

One night, something magical happened. Holly saw a falling star.

As the star trailed across the sky, she made a wish.
"I wish I had a kitten," she whispered.
"A tiny cuddly kitten who could jump in and out of the cat flap."

13

CRASH!

Something big landed on the window sill outside.

It wasn't a kitten . . .

It was Tom, the scruffiest, most raggedy cat Holly had ever seen. He sat there in the moonlight, smiling a crooked smile.

"Miao-o-ow!"

"I'm Tom, your wish cat," he seemed to say.

"It's a mistake," cried Holly.
"I wished for a kitten."
Tom didn't think Holly had
made a mistake.

He rubbed his torn ear
against the window and
howled so loudly it made
him cough and splutter.

"Miao-o-ow, o-o-w, o-o-w!"

Holly hid under her
duvet, hoping that
he'd go away.

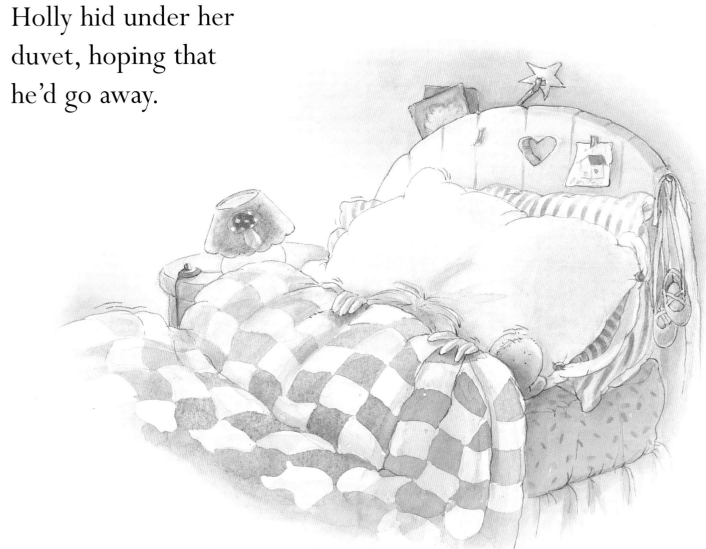

The next morning, Tom was still there, waiting for her outside the cat flap. He wanted to come in, and he had brought her a present of a smelly old piece of fish.

"Yuk!" said Holly. She picked it up and dropped it in the dustbin. Tom looked puzzled. "Bad cat," she said, shooing him away.

"Go on, go home!" said Holly, walking across to her swing.

But Tom was there before her. He sharpened his claws on the swing . . .

and washed his coat noisily, pulling out bits of fur and spitting them everywhere.

At lunchtime, Tom sat on the
window sill, watching Holly eat.

She broke off a piece of her sandwich and
passed it out to him through the cat flap.
Tom wolfed it down, purring all the while.

In the afternoon, a cold wind swept through the garden, and Holly had to wear her jacket and scarf. Tom didn't seem to feel the cold. He followed her around . . .

chasing leaves . . .

balancing along the
top of the fence . . .

showing off.

Soon it was time for Holly
to go indoors to tea.
"Bye then, Tom," she said,
and stroked his tatty head.

26

Tom followed her across to
the door and settled himself
by the cat flap.

That evening, it snowed.
Gleaming pompoms of
snow danced in the air.
Outside the cat flap,
Tom curled himself into a
ragged ball to keep warm.
Soon there was a white
cushion of snow all over
the doorstep, and on Tom.

Holly heard him miaowing miserably.
She ran to the cat flap and held it open . . .

Tom came in, shaking snow all over
the kitchen floor.
"Poor old Tom," said Holly.

He ate a large plate of food, and drank
an even larger bowl of warm milk.
Tom purred louder than ever when
Holly dried him with the kitchen towel.

31

Soon Tom had settled down,
snug on Holly's bed.
Holly stroked his scruffy fur,
and together they watched
the glittering stars.

Then, suddenly, another star
fell. Holly couldn't think of
a single thing to wish for.
She had everything she
wanted. And so had Tom.

The Very Busy Day

Diana Hendry

Jane Chapman

It was a hot sunny day, and Big Mouse was digging in the garden.

SWISH!

Little Mouse sat on the swing, wearing his sun hat. "There's a lot of digging to do," said Big Mouse. "Come and help me, Little Mouse." "I'm too busy to help," said Little Mouse. "I'm dreaming up something."
And he swung up and down, up and down.

"You could put in these seeds,"
said Big Mouse. "If you plant them
in the dark, they'll dream up flowers."

SWISH!

"Umm," said Little
Mouse, "but I've got my
own dream, and I'm busy
thinking about it."
"Busy doing nothing,"
grumbled Big Mouse.

WHEEE!

Little Mouse slid off the swing and jumped into the wheelbarrow. He lay and gazed at the sky. "I need that wheelbarrow for the weeds," said Big Mouse. "And look at all the mess you've made."

Big Mouse tipped Little Mouse
out on to the grass. "Please,
Little Mouse, I need some help."
"I'm far too busy to help," cried
Little Mouse, and he ran off to
pick some daisies.

45

Big Mouse picked up all the
weeds. He mopped his brow
and rubbed his back.
"Phew, it's hot," he puffed . . .

"And this barrow's very
heavy all of a sudden."
It was heavy because Little
Mouse had jumped back in!
He was sitting on top of the
weeds making a daisy chain.

CREAK!

"I'm not pushing you and the weeds," said
Big Mouse indignantly. "Out you get! Come and
help me take the weeds to the rubbish dump."
Little Mouse hung the daisy chain round his
neck and scrambled out of the barrow.

But he didn't help
Big Mouse. He picked
lots and lots of clover
instead. He put the
clover in a flowerpot
on the back doorstep.

HUFF!

PUFF!

Big Mouse pushed the wheelbarrow to
the dump by himself, muttering crossly.

Big Mouse went to find his rake.
He couldn't see Little Mouse anywhere.
"Come on, Little Mouse," he called.
"There's a little rake here
for you too."

POLISH
POLISH
3

51

ON POLISH

52

As Big Mouse climbed down the ladder,
Little Mouse poked his head out. "Can't you
see I'm busy?" he called. "I'm collecting birds'
feathers. This dream is very hard work."
"Humph!" said Big Mouse. "There's
dreaming and there's doing. What
about a little doing from you!"

HUMPH!

Little Mouse had found
three snowy white feathers.
He laid them carefully
on the doorstep.

POLISH

SION POLISH

3

By now, Big Mouse
was busy. "Little Mouse,"
he called. "You could help
me carry this strawberry
down the ladder."
"Can't stop now," said
Little Mouse. "I need
something from the
kitchen."

The sun had made Big
Mouse's head ache, and he
felt very snappy with Little
Mouse for not helping him.
"Whatever's he doing now?"
he grumbled.

MANSION POLISH

Little Mouse rushed out into
the garden. "Big Mouse,
Big Mouse," he called. "Look
what I've made for you!"

57

"It's your very own special sun hat!"
"Oh thank you, Little Mouse," said
Big Mouse, putting it on his head.
"Now I can see why you've been
so busy dreaming. It's my very
special Dream Hat!"

"We've both been very busy,"
said Little Mouse, yawning.
"There's just time to do one
more thing," said Big Mouse.

59

"And that's to have a nice long snooze!" Big Mouse and Little Mouse curled up together underneath the leaves. Little Mouse's hat fell off, and Big Mouse's hat slid right down over his nose.

60

The Most Precious Thing

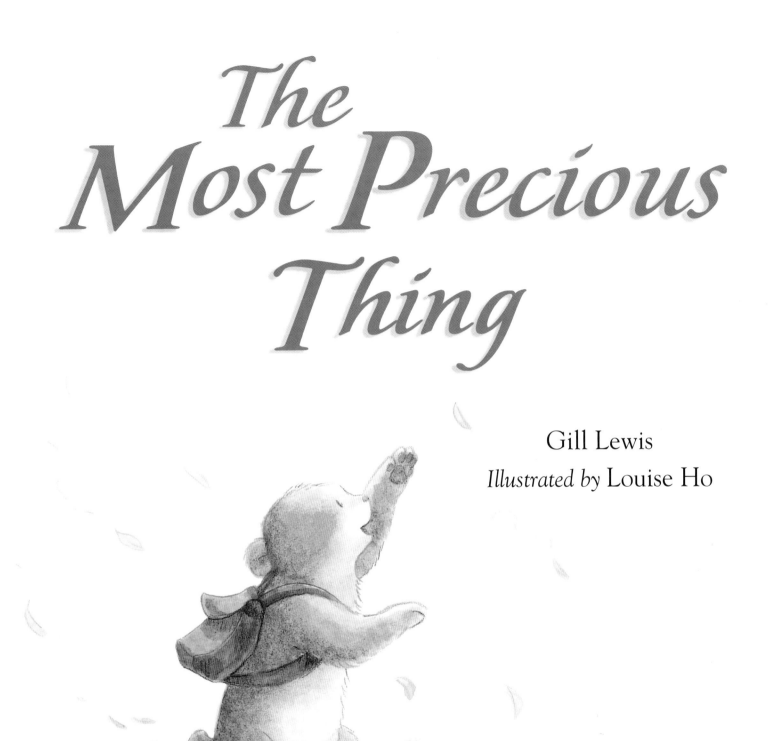

Gill Lewis

Illustrated by Louise Ho

Little Bear was taking Mummy Bear on a walk through the forest in the autumn sunlight. She wanted to show her the special place where the juiciest berries and the sweetest nuts could be found.

As Little Bear skipped through
the rustling leaves, she suddenly
spied a small blue stone glittering
in the sunshine.

"Look, Mummy, look!" cried Little Bear, picking it up. "Look at this shiny jewel I have found."

Little Bear gazed as it sparkled in her paw.

"It must be the most precious thing in the whole wide world," she gasped.

"Oh yes, Little Bear, this is a very beautiful stone," said Mummy Bear, holding it up so that it twinkled in the light, "but the most precious thing is even prettier than this."

"Really?" said Little Bear in wonder. She put the stone carefully in her bag. "Let's go and look! I want to find the most precious thing EVER!"

"Wait for me," laughed Mummy Bear, as Little Bear scampered off through the trees.

Little Bear and Mummy Bear played games
in the afternoon sun. They tried to catch the
seeds that spun in the breeze. And Little
Bear kept looking for something prettier
than the little blue stone.

After a while they came to Little Bear's special place and they filled their tummies with juicy purple blackberries. Little Bear was reaching for a berry when she saw something pink hidden in the brambles . . .

It was a beautiful wild rose.

"Mummy!" shouted Little Bear excitedly. "Come and see what I have found!"

She stroked the rose's silky petals and sniffed its sweet smell. "I've never seen such a pretty flower. Surely this must be the most precious thing?"

"This rose is very pretty, Little Bear," said
Mummy Bear, "and it's soft as velvet." She
tickled the rose against Little Bear's nose,
making her sneeze. "But the most precious
thing is even softer than this."

Little Bear wondered what on earth could be softer than her beautiful rose. She searched and searched through the dry, crunchy leaves, but she found only spiky horse chestnuts, bristly pine cones and a rather cross hedgehog!

Just then she caught sight of something fluttering high up in the trees.

"Look up there!" she shouted. "That *has* to be it!"

Mummy Bear lifted Little Bear up into the air. Caught in a spider's web was a tiny fluffy feather. Little Bear reached up high and took the feather very gently in her paw.

Little Bear touched the downy
feather against her cheek.

"Oh Mummy," she whispered
hopefully. "Please tell me. Is
this the most precious thing?"

"It is very soft," said Mummy
Bear, "but the most precious
thing is even better than this
– it makes me want to dance
for joy."

And Mummy Bear twirled
Little Bear round, making
her giggle.

Little Bear was determined
to find the most precious thing.
She ran up a grassy hilltop to
look out at the woods and
fields. Hundreds of dazzling
butterflies suddenly filled the
air around her.

One of the butterflies landed
lightly on her paw. Little Bear
gazed at it in wonder.

"This is it!" she sang out
happily. "At last I have found
the most precious thing in
the whole of the big
wide world."

Little Bear and Mummy Bear lay in the long grass as the butterfly fluttered through the golden sunlight.

"Oh yes, that is very special," said Mummy Bear softly, "but I can hold the most precious thing safe and tight in my arms."

"Oh, please tell me what it is!" said Little Bear crossly. "I have looked absolutely everywhere and I still haven't found it."

Mummy Bear smiled. "The most precious thing is prettier than any jewel, is softer than a rose or the fluffiest feather, and fills me with more joy than a dancing butterfly. The most precious thing . . ." she said, hugging Little Bear tightly, ". . . is you!"

Mouse, Mole
and the Falling Star

A H Benjamin   John Bendall-Brunello

Mole and Mouse were the best of friends. They had fun together.

They shared everything.

They trusted each other completely, even with their deepest secrets.

When one was sad or not feeling well the other was always there to comfort him.

That's how much they loved each other.
"I'm lucky to have a friend like you," Mole would say.

"No," Mouse would reply.
"I'm lucky to have a friend like *you*!"

One summer evening Mole and Mouse lay side
by side on top of a hill, gazing at the starry sky.
"Aren't stars beautiful?" sighed Mole happily.
"Yes," said Mouse. "And magic, too. They
sometimes fall from the sky, you know. And
if you ever find a fallen star, your wishes will
come true."
"Wow!" said Mole. "Then you could wish for
anything in the world and you would have it."
"That's right," said Mouse dreamily. "Just imagine
that!"

Mole and Mouse fell silent
for a moment, dreaming of
magic stars and all the things
they could wish for.

Just then, a shooting star zipped across the
sky. One moment it was there, and the next
it had gone.

"Did you see that?" gasped Mole, sitting up.

"Yes, I did," cried Mouse. "It's a fallen star,
and I'm going to find it!"

Mouse scrambled to his feet and
scurried quickly down the hill.
"Wait!" called Mole, racing after him.
"It's my star! I saw it first."
"No, I saw it first!" shouted Mouse.
"It's *my* star!"

When they reached the bottom of the hill,
Mole and Mouse started searching for the
fallen star. Each one hoped he would find
it first. But neither did.

"Perhaps the star fell in the woods," thought Mouse. "I'll go and look for it tomorrow."

Mole stared towards the woods, too. He was thinking exactly the same.

But they did not tell each other,
and they went back to their homes,
without even saying goodnight.

The next day before sunrise, Mole sneaked out of his house and set off towards the woods.

A few minutes later, Mouse did the same.

Mouse and Mole spent the whole morning in the woods,
looking for the fallen star. Once or twice, they spotted
each other. But they pretended they hadn't.

Then, towards afternoon, Mole came across a small patch of charred grass.

"Maybe this is where the star has fallen," he thought.

"But someone's already taken it. It can only be Mouse!"

A little later, Mouse came across the same charred
patch of grass. He thought the star had fallen there, too.
"It's gone!" he cried. "And I bet I know who's taken it.
It has to be Mole!"

As darkness fell, both Mole and Mouse made their separate ways home, each feeling very angry with the other. They did not speak to each other again, except to argue.

"You stole my star!" Mole yelled.
"No, *you* stole *my* star!" Mouse
yelled back.
Mole didn't trust Mouse and
Mouse didn't trust Mole.

So, Mole sneaked into Mouse's house to find the star . . .

110

and later on Mouse looked through
Mole's window to see where Mole
had hidden it.
But neither found the fallen star.

The days rolled by and summer was nearly
over. Mole and Mouse grew lonely and miserable.
They missed each other's company, the fun they
used to have together, the secrets they had shared.
They even missed the sad moments.

"Mole can keep the star if he wants," thought Mouse.
"All I want is my friend back."
"If I had never seen that star, Mouse would
still be my friend," thought Mole.

Soon the fallen star became
just a sad memory – until
one day . . .

Mouse was climbing up the hill when
he spotted a golden leaf, swirling and
twirling in the air.
"It's the fallen star!" he cried. "Mole
must have lost it. I'll catch it for him."
Not far away Mole noticed Mouse
chasing after something that looked
very like a star.
"It's Mouse's star," he thought.
"I'll help him catch it."

Up and up the hill ran Mole and
Mouse, until they reached the top.
But the leaf was already high in
the sky, glimmering in the autumn
sunshine. It swayed this way and
that, as if waving goodbye, and
then vanished altogether.

"The star has gone back to the sky," said Mouse.
"That's where it belongs," said Mole.
"Maybe it's for the best," sighed Mouse.
"I'm sure it is," agreed Mole.
There was a moment's silence.
"Anyway, we don't need a star.
We have each other," said Mouse.
"Of course we have," agreed Mole.

They gave each other a big hug, then they lay back on top of the hill, feeling the wind. With their arms and legs stretched out, they looked just like two furry stars.